The COLOR of My WORDS

LYNN JOSEPH

JOANNA COTLER BOOKS

HarperTrophy®
An Imprint of HarperCollinsPublishers

Harper Trophy® is a registered trademark of
HarperCollins Publishers Inc.

The Color of My Words
Copyright © 2000 by Lynn Joseph

Printed in the United States of America. For information address
HarperCollins Children's Books, a division of HarperCollins Publishers,
1350 Avenue of the Americas, New York, NY 10019.

Library of Congress Cataloging-in-Publication Data
Joseph, Lynn.
  The color of my words / by Lynn Joseph.
    p.   cm.
  "Joanna Cotler books."
  Summary: When life gets difficult for Ana Rosa, a twelve-year-old would-be
writer living in a small village in the Dominican Republic, she can depend on
her older brother to make her feel better—until the life-changing events on her
thirteenth birthday.
  ISBN 0-06-028232-0 — ISBN 0-06-028233-9 (lib. bdg.)
  ISBN 0-06-447204-3 (pbk.)
  [1. Family life—Dominican Republic—Fiction.   2. Brothers and sisters—
Fiction.   3. Dominican Republic—Fiction.]   I. Title.
PZ7.J77935 Co   2000   00-22440
[Fic]—dc21   CIP
                                                                   AC

Typography by Alicia Mikles
❖
First Harper Trophy edition, 2002

Visit us on the World Wide Web!
www.harperchildrens.com

For my sons, Jared and Brandt:
You share my love for the Dominican Republic—
the friends we made, the beautiful beaches—
but, there is much more to see, guys,
and we'll see it together!

and

For Angel Hèrnandez:
You inspired every word of this book.
Thank you for sharing the stories
of your life with me. I hope you find
the future you're searching for.

SOMETIMES YOU HAVE NO CONTROL over what will happen next, as I discovered the year I was twelve years old—but sometimes you do. And when you do, that's when it is time to take charge because you sure don't know when the chance will come again.

～

WASH DAY

Saturday is wash day for Mami and me
down by the river that flows to the sea.
We carry the baskets high on our hips.
We juggle the soap, the scrub board, and clips.

Our friends wave hola as we slippery-slide
On river-age stones to the other side.
Where sun rays glimmer on a whisper of shade.
And Mami and me tie our hair up in braids.

Then WHACK! I smack the clothes on the rocks
to scare out all dirt and grassy spots.
Mami scrubs them up and down,
and we both swirl them round and round.

Sparkling white, and river clean
the clothes smell like fresh-air dreams.
We clip them safe to bushes and trees
to dry in the sun and flap in the breeze.

Later, under the moon's blue light
Mami and me smooth the wrinkled clothes right.
We fold them into neat little squares
And take them back home for all to wear.

WASH DAY WAS THE DAY I'D get Mami all to myself. For me it was the best day of the week. Unless it rained. Then I'd have to keep on sharing Mami with everyone, especially Papi, who sat on the porch and never moved. Mami had no time to pat her hair down, let alone share private thoughts the way we did on wash day.

At the river's edge, I'd tell Mami all the special things I had thought about during the week. If I wrote a new poem, I would recite it to her while we dipped our hands into the cool water. It was just me and her and the river. No other hands, no other ears.

Mami was the only person who knew I wanted to write books when I grew up. I knew it was a strange thing to want to do, because we sure didn't know any writers around here. In fact, Papi told me that in the República Dominicana, only the President could write books.

I think it's true. I went to the *librería* and I saw a lot of books by President Balaguer. I told Mami this during one wash day. We were pounding the clothes with rocks, and I gripped mine hard as I beat the dirt out of Papi's overalls and my brother Guario's waiter uniforms.

Mami didn't say anything. She just kept turning her sheet over and over as she pounded away. Finally she looked up and said, "Ana Rosa, there always has to be a first person to do something."

I think Mami was telling me that there was no reason why I couldn't try and be the first writer who wasn't President of our

Island. Either that or she was hinting that I should run for President, and then if I won I could write what I wanted.

Sometimes Mami's words are a puzzle. I have to spin them around and around in my head as if I am doing a mental *merengue*. Sooner or later I figure out the dance, but sometimes I wish she would just say what she means straight out.

Papi might sound as if he is talking in a puzzle, but I always know exactly what he means. Like when I asked him if I could have a notebook just for writing my poems in. He said, "Muchacha, your head is getting bigger than your hat."

When I told Mami this on our next wash day, she laughed. But I could tell the laugh was only in her throat and not in her heart.

"Your papi says funny things sometimes, *cariño*," she said. "He's a dreamer."

"A dreamer?" I asked. "How can you

say that, Mami? All Papi does is sit on the porch and drink rum."

Mami's hand shot out faster than a lizard under a rock. I felt the pain on my cheek before I realized what had happened.

"You have no hair on your tongue, *chica*. Be careful!"

I swallowed my tears and beat the clothes harder. Wash day had never been a day of sharp words and slaps. I felt as if Papi was a rock falling down from the hills and into our river. After the big splash, there was nothing but silence.

In daylight, silence is louder and angrier than at any other time. There are no sweet measures of silence such as night's stars, or evening's sunset, or morning's growing light. There is only bright, hard silence and it sounds louder than drums.

I glanced over at Mami. She was dipping the clothes into the river. "Look, Ana Rosa," she said. "Look at the river."

I looked. The water rushed around Mami's brown knees and through her blistered red fingers, leaving wet kisses on her skin.

"It'll never pass this way again," she said. "Off it will go down to the sea, where it will foam with the waves and swim with the fish and glide ships along on steady or rough courses depending on its mood. Around and around the world it will go, this water that slips by me so quickly. Far from the República Dominicana, far from me, but always under the same sky and sun."

I had never heard Mami say so much at one time. I looked closely at the river but I could not see all that she saw in it.

"You are this river, Ana Rosa," she whispered. "But you must flow softly around the rocks on your way to meet the sea. There you can do as you wish."

Mami's words were gentle. But her

brown eyes were slits of worry like moon slices on a dark night. There was no happiness in the smile she gave me.

Many days and nights I thought about Mami's words. But no matter how I turned them or shook them or chased them from my mind, they always came back telling me the same thing. Mami was scared.

Mami did not have to tell me what everyone on my Island knows. And what I know, too.

Writers have died here. At least those brave enough to hurl words at our government.

"But Mami," I whispered as I hugged the wall between my bed and hers, "I write poems and stories."

And in the hot, sticky darkness, I heard Mami's answer, "Sometimes it is better to keep those things inside—for a while."

I was right. She was warning me to keep quiet. To wait until I left the Island

and could write what I wanted. When I didn't live in a country where silence was self-defense.

But I wanted to shake Mami's eyes open. Would we always be silent—the bright, hard daylight kind that is louder than drums? Couldn't I say what I wished—on paper? Even if it is only that Papi sits on the porch all day drinking rum? There! I shall never say it out loud again. Mami's slap will last a lifetime. What if I write what I want while I am still a river flowing around the rocks in my Island?

As Mami herself said, there always has to be a first person to do something.

WORDS

May I have some paper, please
Please, may I have some paper
'Cause these words of mine
go walk away
they go walk away all by themselves
and get lost in the crowd.

May I have some paper, please
Please, may I have some paper
To catch these words
and wrap them up
where they can't walk away
slip off the edge
and drown.

I WAS TURNING INTO A LITTLE THIEF—always stealing bits and pieces of paper to write on. Sometimes it was the paper bags that Papi brought home his bottles of rum in. Sometimes napkins or the gray paper that the shopkeepers use to wrap up goods. But I wanted more than anything a notepad of my very own. One in which I could write "POEMS by Ana Rosa Hèrnandez" on the first page and then fill it up with words—long words, short words, words that smelled and tasted and felt like something new.

But my only notebook was for school. Mami told me that a new notebook cost 40 pesos—a lot of money—two whole dinners for our family. How many bottles of rum can Papi buy with 40 pesos, I wondered.

My brother Guario had a notepad. It was filled with pages of empty spaces waiting for words. I asked him once, "Guario, can I have your notepad to write my poems in?"

He shook his head. "It's for work, *cara*. I'm sorry. But you can tell me your poems anytime you want."

I looked up at my big brother and smiled.

Guario worked as a waiter at a restaurant near the beach. Everyone knew that Guario had one of the best jobs in town because he was very handsome. The tourists liked to have him smile and chat with them while they ordered their food. Girls from cold, faraway countries were always falling in love with my brother. They touched his dark curly hair and listened to him call them *"mi amor."*

One Friday night, Guario went rushing out of the house to meet his best friend, Angel. They were going to a club to dance *bachatas* and Guario left his notepad sitting on the table. I was alone in the house. Mami had gone out to visit a neighbor. Papi was down at the *colmado* playing dominoes. Roberto and Angela were nowhere around.

Suddenly a breeze swirled through the house and flipped open the cover of Guario's notepad. The empty pages filled with wind and blew up one after the other, showing me all the lovely blank spaces waiting for words. I could write on a few pages and tear them out, I thought. Guario would never notice. I picked up a pencil and looked around. No one was coming.

So I wrote. First one page, then another and another. I stopped when I had filled five pages with words about Mount Isabel de Torres, and about Sosúa Beach, which I love. I wrote about the *niños*, and about climbing my favorite gri gri tree. I wrote a poem about Angela, my beautiful, silly older sister who knew nothing but how to smile at men passing by our porch. I wrote about my brother Roberto who worked hard in the sun renting beach chairs to tourists. Suddenly the lights went out. It was another power blackout. A good thing, too, because I might not have stopped writing.

I tore out the pages carefully and slipped them into my pocket. I went and sat on the porch and watched as the sky filled up its blue spaces with pinks and oranges and a deep, deep purple. Utter darkness swelled over everything. With the darkness was complete silence as well since the neighbors' radios could not blare out their loud *merengues*.

I felt the pages in my pocket. Just a couple more, I thought. No one would know at all. I tiptoed back inside and lit a candle. I sat at the table and wrote under the candle's light. I wrote one page after another until there were no more empty pages in Guario's notebook.

Then I heard a noise.

"Ana Rosa, are you there?"

It was Mami. I jumped up and stuffed the notepad into my pocket.

"*Sí*, Mami. Right here."

"What are you doing, *cariño*?" she asked.

"*Nada*, Mami, *nada*!" I said loudly to chase away the shakings in my body.

Mami came over and put her hand under my chin. She tilted my head toward the candle's light and looked into my eyes. "You sure?" she asked.

I nodded and swallowed. I put my hand over the notepad in my pocket and slipped out of the room. I went into the bedroom that I shared with Angela. I sat on the bed with my hand in my pocket, holding my secret close. Finally I reached under the thin mattress and stuffed the notepad as close to my side of the bed as I could.

The next day, everybody in the house was looking for that notepad. Guario was shouting that he would be fired. That made Papi very frightened. Although Papi always swore that if he got up off his porch chair in the middle of the day, he'd get heatstroke, he, too, was helping to look for the book.

It was like a madhouse. Papi and Guario and Roberto and Angela and my little cousins were throwing everything out the front door in their frantic search. Chairs, a radio, empty rum bottles, old newspapers, clothes, shoes, our two dogs, some stray hens pecking at this and that, all went sailing into the dusty yard.

Of course, I knew exactly where it was—under the mattress—but I was too scared to say so. I pretended to help look around the house. Then I went into the kitchen where Mami was rolling out dough for *empanadas*.

"Mami," I said nervously, "everyone's looking for Guario's notepad."

Mami nodded her head but didn't look up. I only had to stand there for a minute before she said, "It will turn up when it's ready."

That's when I knew that she knew. I waited for her to shout at me, but Mami just kept on sprinkling flour and rolling the dough. I just didn't understand Mami at all.

I went into the bedroom and slipped my hand far under the mattress. The notepad was there. I sat on the floor chewing on my finger. Guario had already asked

me twice if I had seen his notepad and I
had said no.

I couldn't stop how fast the no came
out my mouth. I wanted to tell him the
truth, but my mouth just wouldn't say anything else.

"What are you doing just sitting
there?" asked Angela, coming into the bedroom. She tossed pillows on the floor and
started to pull the sheets off the bed.

"I looked there already," I said quickly,
before she decided to turn the mattress
upside down.

My heart was beating faster and faster
as Guario's shouting filled up all corners of
the house. Papi was cursing and Roberto
and Angela were racing around with scared
looks on their faces. There was a horrible
fear in the air—fear of what would happen
if Guario lost his job. There was no way in
the world I could hand over that notepad

now with every page of it full of my care-less words.

Then we heard Mami's voice. "Lunch is ready. Come inside and eat. And stop fuss-ing about that notepad." The stern sound covered me like night's sweet darkness. Mami knew and she wasn't telling.

Now, no matter what is wrong in our family, we always listen to Mami. So when Mami called us all to eat, we stopped our wild hunting and sat down at the table. Papi said the prayer and Mami served us plates full of red beans and rice and crispy, brown *empanadas* stuffed with chicken and spices. There were tall glasses of lime juice and precious ice cubes.

It was one of the best lunches ever and it could have been served for a holiday. It was as if Mami had cooked this special meal on purpose to distract the family. And it worked. Afterward everyone sat back, full and relaxed, as if *empanadas* could make the world look brighter and red beans and rice made worries disappear.

We talked about where the notepad could be and what could have happened to it. Papi wasn't cursing anymore and Guario wasn't shouting.

Finally Papi reached into his pocket and took out some pesos. He put them on the table. Then Mami dug her hand deep into a pocket of her dress and put some pesos on the table, too. Roberto jumped up and went into the kitchen and came back with some pesos that he put next to Papi's and Mami's pesos. Guario looked surprised and I noticed that his eyes were turning bright red as if he were trying not to cry.

But that could not be possible. I had never seen Guario cry in my life. Guario was nineteen years old and he was my big, strong brother who took care of everything. Mami called him *Jefe* when Papi was not around. *Jefe* means "boss" and that is what Guario was. He worked two jobs and bought all our food and fixed everything that went wrong. He was always serious.

"Here," said Papi, pushing the pesos over to Guario, "take this and buy a new notepad for work."

Guario nodded and stood up. He walked around the table and kissed Mami on her cheek. Then he walked out the house to go to work.

I watched Guario's wide back move steadily away from us. When I turned around, Mami raised her eyebrows at me as if to say "What are you waiting for?"

I jumped up and ran after Guario. He was at the corner waiting for one of the noisy motorcycle taxis to take him to work.

"Guario," I called.

He turned around. I dashed up to him and threw my arms around his waist.

His hand smoothed down the flyaway hairs in my ponytail.

"I took your notepad," I whispered into his shirt. "I'm sorry."

Guario kept stroking my hair. After a while, he said, "I know what it feels like."

"How what feels like?" I asked.

"To want something so bad."

"What have you wanted so bad?" I asked, looking up at him.

"A future," he answered. And then I saw the tears in his eyes for real. This was not the first time I had heard Guario talk about wanting a future. I just never paid it any attention. But to be right there at that moment hearing and seeing him, the whole world tilted for the first time away from me, me, me to someone else—my big brother.

Guario and I stood at the corner with our arms around each other as all the motorcycle taxis drove by blowing their horns. It was the first time I knew that words could not tell everything.

THE
GRI GRI TREE

I like to sit high
in my gri gri tree
where I can survey
all below me.

On top of the gri gri
I'm a strong, dark queen
sitting on a throne
of towering green.

I hold the leaves close
as the wind blows past.
I kiss the rain drops
as the thunder blasts.

I'm the gri gri queen
and I'm in command
protecting my tree
from careless hands.

Alone with a treasure
no one else sees.
Hidden from the world
and all who seek me.

N O ONE HAD TO POINT OUT THAT I was different from everyone else in our village. It was clear from the first day I began climbing the gri gri tree and staying up there for hours.

"What's wrong with your daughter?" neighbors asked Mami.

"She's not right in her head," they answered themselves, when Mami only shrugged her shoulders.

Papi would say, "Nothing wrong with sitting in a tree. It's the same as sitting on a porch except it's higher."

Roberto would climb up with me sometimes but he got bored quickly and swung down, yelling like a monkey. Angela shook her head at me and said I would never be a real *chica*, because *chicas* do not climb trees when they are twelve years old.

Not even Guario understood, although he tried. He asked me once what I did up there. That was more than anyone else had ventured to inquire.

I told him I looked around.

He asked if I didn't think I was wasting a lot of time, when I could be doing something to prepare for my future such as studying English.

Guario always had his mind on the future. Sometimes I think that he was tormented by all of us who didn't particularly care what tomorrow was going to bring. And really, what was there to know— either it would rain or it would not. But it was definitely going to be hot and Mami was going to cook and Papi was going to sit on the porch and the radio was going to play *merengues* all day. That was for sure.

Besides, I already knew what I wanted to do in my future. I wanted to be a writer, but only Mami knew that. If I told Guario, he would say I was unreasonable. If I told anyone else, they would laugh. But in my gri gri tree, I could be anything I wanted to be—even a writer with words for everything I saw from my leafy green hideout.

I could see the ocean glittering silver in the sunlight. I could see people trudging along the dusty road from Sosúa; some balancing buckets of water on their heads. I could see boys playing baseball in the schoolyard with a tree branch bat and a rubber band ball. I could see the river, meandering over rocks, hungry for rain. Far off in Puerto Plata, I could see Mount Isabel de Torres, a green giant with misty white curls dancing 'round her head.

I could see the sleepy lagoon and the sad little homes of the lagoon people. I could see the birds that flew past my gri

gri, their ruby-and-gold velvet feathers shimmering on their tiny bodies. I could see the rainbows that glowed in the sea-sky after a rain passed. I could count the sunset roses in Señora Garcia's backyard. I could see my teacher climbing the hill near her house, and I could see Papi sitting on our porch, nodding off to sleep.

Then one day I saw something that I had never seen before and I was so scared that I almost fell out of the tree. There I was looking at the sea when suddenly out of it rose a giant monster, tall and black and covering the sun with its shadow. Before I could scream, the monster fell back into the sea.

I scrambled down the tree quickly and ran toward my house, shouting "Papi, there's a monster in the sea!"

Papi woke up from his siesta. "*¿Qué pasa?*"

"A monster," I repeated. "A giant sea

monster and it's coming this way!"

I shouted inside the house. "Mami, come quick. There's a monster in the sea. I saw it."

Mami came outside and Angela followed her. They were drying their hands from washing the lunch dishes.

Everyone looked at me as if I were crazy.

"It's true," I said, jumping up and down.

Mami made me sit down and describe exactly what I saw. Before I had finished, Angela shouted my news to her best friend walking by. Then Papi waved over some of his domino-playing *amigos* and told them what I saw from on top of my gri gri tree.

Soon our porch was surrounded with people all asking me to tell my story again.

When I had told it for the fourth time, Señor Garcia, the *colmado* owner, began to laugh.

"You must have fallen asleep in the tree and had a bad dream, *cariño*," he said.

"No," I replied, shaking my head. "I saw it."

But his words had relieved everyone's fears of a sea monster. "Yes," they agreed. "You must have imagined it."

"No, you idiots," I wanted to shout. "I didn't imagine anything." But I kept quiet because Mami and Papi would not like it if I shouted at the neighbors and called them idiots. That was for sure.

As everyone sat down on the porch to share a drink and talk about my sea monster, I slipped away and ran to my gri gri tree. I heard Mami calling me, but I pretended I didn't hear and climbed up the tree fast. I needed to find out if what I had seen would come back again.

I sat down on my usual branch and tucked a few leaves away from my eyes. Then I stared at the sea. I looked so hard and for so long that its blueness filled up my eyeballs and I had to blink a lot so I wouldn't go blind.

The afternoon faded into evening and the sea's blueness turned gray. I watched and waited. My stomach made grumbling noises but I covered them with my hand.

Then, just as I began to think that maybe I had imagined it after all, I saw a splash of white water. The splash of water rose up, up until it was high in the air like a magic fountain.

"It's a volcano," I whispered. I remembered that my teacher had told us how many of the Caribbean islands had been formed by volcanoes that rose out of the sea.

I gasped. Maybe I was seeing the beginning of a brand-new island right next to the República Dominicana. As I kept on looking, a black shape emerged out of the fountain of water. It rose and turned, as if doing a dance, and that's when I saw the gleaming white throat of the sea monster.

It hovered in between heaven and ocean for a few seconds and then fell back into the water with a splash that sprayed salt drops as high as the pearl-pink clouds.

My heart beat furiously and I steadied myself so I wouldn't fall down from the tree. I was right. I had not imagined anything. There really was a sea monster out there. But this time I didn't rush down to tell anyone.

What would the people do, I wondered. Would they try to find it? Or maybe to kill it? Somehow, although I didn't know why, I could tell that the sea monster was not dangerous. It just wanted to swim and splash and jump out of the sea the same way I jumped over the waves.

I climbed down the tree and went home. The first thing I wanted to do was eat, but people were all over the porch talking wildly. "We saw it, Ana Rosa," they shouted. "We saw that big sea monster of yours."

Papi was busy handing out glasses, cups, and small jars, anything that could hold a spot of rum and Coke. Mami was passing around a plate of *dulces*, the sweet milk candy that I love. She must have just made them because they were still warm and soft.

Children were carrying huge plates filled with different foods that their mothers had made. Angela was directing them to put the food here or there on our big table. I saw plates piled high with *arroz con pollo, plátanos fritos,* and *batatas fritas.*

Señor Garcia apologized over and over to me. About a hundred people were gathered on our porch, in the yard, and along the roadside, talking about the sea monster.

"The tourist high-season is coming,"

said Señor Rojas, who owned a Jeep that he rented to tourists. "We can't let anyone know we have a sea monster hanging around Sosúa Bay."

"But why not?" asked Señora Perez, who sold paintings on the beach. "It could be a tourist attraction. Plenty people may decide to come here just to see it."

Half the folks whispered, "He's right." And the other half said, "She's the one who's right."

It looked as if we were going to have a big debate on our porch just like the ones that take place when it is a presidential election year. The way everyone was carrying on, soon we would have people writing *merengues* about the sea monster and there would be sea monster fiestas all over the place just like during elections.

I shook my head and just listened to everyone as I ate a plate heaped high with food. That poor sea monster, I thought.

Then the people began to make a Plan. When Dominicans get together and decide to make a plan, watch out, because there are plans, and then there are Plans, and this was definitely a PLAN!

The first thing the people decided was that someone had to keep watch over this sea monster. Well, everyone looked around to see who would volunteer. That's when we knew the PLAN would not work because no one wanted to do something so stupid as to go down to the sea and watch for the sea monster.

It was Angela who got the bright idea that since I saw it first, I could keep watch over it from my gri gri tree. Everyone turned to me and nodded their heads.

"Finally, a good reason for her to be up there all the time," I heard Señora Garcia whisper.

Papi was looking at me and nodding his head, proud that his daughter was selected for such an important job. I said, Okay, I would do it.

Then the PLAN continued. Half the people wanted to make signs and announce that Sosúa Bay had a new visitor and it was a one-of-a-kind sea monster. The other half of the crowd shook their heads and said, No, it was too obvious.

"We must be subtle about a delicate matter like this," said Señora Perez. "We must make up a wonderful story about this sea monster, give it a name, make it a friendly monster, and then tell the world. Otherwise all we will do is scare everyone away from this side of the island."

She had a point. A story about the sea monster was much better than a big billboard with an arrow pointing "This way to Sea Monster of Sosúa Bay!"

The idea of it all made me giggle. Wait until Guario came home and heard all this. I could hardly wait for him to return from the restaurant.

"Well," said Señor Rojas, "what will we name the sea monster?"

"And who knows how to write a story about it, anyway?" asked Señor Garcia.

Señora Perez shrugged her shoulders. "I don't know how to write too good, but we could make up something."

Then Mami, who was usually quiet during these kinds of discussions, spoke up loud and clear. "Ana Rosa would be the best person to write a story about the sea monster."

I was shocked. This wasn't the same Mami who worshiped silence.

People began to shake their heads. "A child to do something so important?" they whispered.

"Yes," said Mami. "Let us give her a notebook to write in and she will write us a story about the sea monster. If we don't like it, someone else can try."

The way Mami said it, so definite and firm, made people nod their heads in agreement. "Well, it doesn't hurt to let her try," they said.

So Señor Garcia went and brought back a notebook from his *colmado*. Mami gave it to me and her hands were cold like the river.

While the grown-ups stayed up late on the porch talking and drinking and eating, I went inside and began to write a story about the sea monster. First I tried to give him a name. But I couldn't think of a good one. So instead I thought about what he looked like. Then I imagined what he must feel like living all alone in the sea, different from all of the other sea creatures.

The fish and animals in the ocean were probably afraid of his huge size and his big nose and long, swishing tail. And they probably didn't want to play with him.

Maybe they whispered about how strange he looked. But the sea monster wanted a friend. Deep down, I understood exactly how the sea monster must feel.

I began to write. I wrote page after page in the notebook the people had given to me. When I was finished, it was almost midnight. I went to the porch. Everyone was still there laughing and talking and some were dancing to the music on the radio.

Children were asleep on their mothers' and fathers' laps. Some of the bigger children were sprawled out on a blanket on the floor and the *merengue* music was a background lullaby for them.

When the people saw me, they got quiet. Someone turned off the radio. Some woke the children on their laps. Papi moved from his chair and put his arm around my shoulders. He led me to the front of the porch.

Then everyone watched me and waited. I stood there trembling, holding that notebook with my story close to my heart. I knew right then that this was it. The whole world would find out about me.

I stopped thinking. I just started to read. I did not look at anyone, not Papi, or Mami or Angela. I read and read until I turned to the last page of the story. There the other sea creatures invite the lonely sea monster to a big underwater fiesta, even though there is no one else like him around, and even though he is so big that he knocks over many of them with his big nose and tail.

"And the sea monster is so happy that he leaps out of the ocean, sending sparkling waves all around him in a giant ring of light."

I looked up then and I saw many things at once. I saw Papi sitting on the edge of his chair, strange and silent. I saw

Mami with her hands folded and her head bowed as if praying. I saw the neighbors smiling and nodding their heads. Then I saw Guario, who must have walked up to the edge of the porch while I was reading.

It was Guario's face I focused on. He was smiling. My big strong brother who worried about our future, my serious Guario who almost never smiled, suddenly let out a loud whoop and grabbed me up. He spun me around and around.

"Little sister, I am buying you a new notebook every month no matter what!" he shouted.

I closed my eyes so I wouldn't start crying there in front of all the neighbors. Guario always kept his promises. I would be able to write down everything now, everything I thought or dreamed or felt or saw or wondered about. I was so happy I thought I would leap as high as the sea monster.

Then, in the background, I heard clapping. The people had stood up from their chairs and were clapping for me.

I heard shouts of how great my story was and people congratulating Papi and kissing Mami's cheeks telling them how lucky it was that I was so smart. I heard Mami saying it had nothing to do with luck. I grinned and went over to her. She put her arm around me and squeezed my shoulders.

"You're going to write many stories, remember, *cara*?" she whispered in my ear. It was the happiest night in my life.

We all forgot about the sea monster until the next day.

Over the radio, a news broadcast announced that one of the humpback whales making its way to Samaná Bay for the annual winter mating season had gotten sidetracked in Sosúa.

"But Samaná Bay is only a two-hour

drive from here," said Papi.

"Well, the poor whale doesn't know how to drive," Mami teased.

For two weeks our humpback whale jumped and frolicked about in Sosúa Bay until finally heading east to Samaná to join the other three thousand humpbacks that go there every winter.

But while he was in Sosúa, I watched him every day from my gri gri tree. The beautiful black-and-white sea monster had helped me to make my dream come true. I loved the whale. And I named him Guario.

MERENGUE DREAM

I turn to the right
I turn to the left
I twirl a circle moon
in my merengue dream.

I tap to the front
I tap to the back
I shimmy with the stars
in my merengue dream.

I spin to the east
I spin to the west
I dance across the night
in my merengue dream.

I open my eyes
I tremble and slide
My knees start to buckle
and my dreams subside.

IN THE REPÚBLICA DOMINICANA, music grows in our blood right from the cradle, and dancing bleeds it out in bold colors, reds and purples, swirling everywhere. We wake up to *merengue* and go to sleep to sweet *salsa*. In between we sway and sigh to the melancholy sounds of countryside *bachata*.

In our neighborhood wooden houses are set side by side in every color of the rainbow. Our radios are perched like black birds on our porches to warn passersby that someone is at home and to pick up your feet. At night the *merengue* is loud enough to shake the stars right out of the sky.

Here no one loves to dance more than my Papi. *Merengue, bachata, salsa*—all of these dances Papi can do with such grace that watching him step and spin and glide across the porch makes you think that the music is floating from the air straight to his feet.

Twice a month, on Guario's paydays, we have a small fiesta on our porch. Mami makes a big pot of *sancocho* with juicy pieces of pork and chicken and lots of yucca and *plátanos* all stirred up in a nice stew. I sit on the floor peeling about one hundred *chinas*, the sweetest oranges ever, to make orange juice. By the time I am finished I am surrounded by a pyramid of orange peel that creeps around me in circles up to my neck.

Papi sets up seats on the porch. Any chair or even a wooden board that could be balanced on two cement blocks would do. Papi sends Roberto down to the *colmado* to buy bottles of Brugal rum and Cokes. Then Papi bathes in the river and comes back looking sparkling clean with a fresh shirt and pants and his dark curly hair slicked down so fine that you could see the comb's teeth marks in it.

By the time the fiesta starts, though, Papi's hair would be in curls all over his head again, each curl springing up separately, a rebellion of his primary African race over his Spanish bloodline.

I loved and hated these fiestas. I loved them because everyone was happy and called me *mi amor*, *linda*, and *cariño* for the rest of the day. It was as if God's angels were hovering low over the Island. On fiesta days, people forgot their roofs that leaked rain, and the jobs that were closing down, and the tourists that didn't come this year, and how much they missed husbands and brothers who worked hard in *Nueva* York and sent money home by Western Union. On fiesta days, there were no *problemas*!

The reason I hated the fiestas was because I was the only person on this Island who couldn't dance. Believe me, I tried. Sometimes I spun the wrong way, sometimes too fast, and almost fell, sometimes I turned and couldn't find my partner, who was looking for me in another direction.

In my dreams I could dance like a fairy, smooth and beautiful, with dresses that floated around my knees. But on our front porch I was like a fish washed up on the sand. No matter how hard I flipped and flapped, I wasn't going anywhere.

The worst part was that people would say, "But you can't be *la hija* of Señor Hèrnandez. He dances like the wind. What is wrong with you?"

Instead of dancing I would hide behind the wooden table, which teetered under the tremendous weight of Mami's *sancocho* and our neighbors' pots full of *arroz con pollo*. I served food to everyone who stopped by. I poured glasses of juice. I changed cassettes in the radio. I held the babies on my lap and sang the songs to them. And I watched. To see if I could learn the secret to dancing.

I watched closely as Papi tucked a red hibiscus behind Mami's ear and whirled her around and around the porch. Mami's feet flew in between Papi's legs, never seeming to touch the porch. They slid in then out, then around, then to the left and to the right and around in twirls, flying across the porch as if weaving starlight from musical dust.

And Papi—he was a different person completely. He was no longer the loud voice in a porch chair. He was the angel of dance. He was the blue moon shimmering in the night sky. He was a laughing, handsome man, almost as handsome as Guario. Everyone stared at him as if they couldn't believe that Señor Hèrnandez was human and not a star that had fallen down and decided to have some fun before ascending back to the sky. He was everything that was mystery and magic and it was during these fiestas that I loved my Papi so much that I could see what Mami saw—a dreamer, not a drinker—a dancer, not a drunk.

Then came the night of the fiesta that Papi stopped in the middle of a song and looked right at me. He held out his hand like a prince.

"Come, *muchacha*, dance with your Papi."

I shook my head. My cheeks were hot with shame. The shame filled my body, making my bare toes tingle.

Papi looked at me for a few more moments. I was probably the only person who had ever refused to dance with him.

The next morning, Papi did not sit on his porch chair after breakfast. Instead he dressed in a nice pair of pants and he said to me, "Come, Ana Rosa. Today you will learn how to dance."

"Papi, I don't like to dance," I mumbled, as I washed the dishes.

Papi snorted out loud. "You hear that, God," he said, looking up at the galvanized roof of our house. "She doesn't like to dance."

Then he looked at me. "Only fools don't love what God gives so freely."

It was the first time that Papi had spoken to me like this. Usually he asked me to bring him a glass, or some ice, or a plate of food. Sometimes, when he was happy with two drinks in his belly, he laughed and pulled my ponytail as I walked by.

But this morning, he hadn't had any drinks as yet, and he was looking mighty serious. As serious as Guario.

"Put on your shoes, Ana Rosa," Papi insisted. "We are going to dance."

At first Papi put on a *merengue*, but he decided it was too fast. Then he put on other *merengues*. Slower ones, snappier ones, funny ones. None of them worked. My hips switched when they should sway. And my knees bucked in and out like a jerky puppet's. We moved from the front porch to the side yard where no one could see us.

"Feel the music, Ana Rosa," said Papi.

"I don't know how, Papi," I wailed. "It's not a tree or a flower. It's like trying to feel the sea. It keeps slipping away."

"Then listen to the words," Papi persisted. "You love words; listen and dance to them."

It sounded like good advice, but for once I realized that words could not help me. I could not dance to words any easier than I could to the rhythm that seeped so secretly into everyone but me.

All morning Papi tried to teach me to dance but the harder he tried, the more my feet tangled with his.

"It's no use, Papi," I said, almost in tears.

"Give up, Papi," said Angela, who was watching us from the kitchen window.

"Nunca," said Papi. "She will learn. We just have to find a way for her to feel the music."

Then Papi stopped just so in the middle of the yard and I almost tripped and fell.

"What's the matter?" I asked.

"Ana Rosa," whispered Papi, "do you even *like* the music?"

The look on Papi's face would have made me laugh if I were not so miserable.

"*Sí*, Papi, *sí*," I said. "I love the music."

Papi's shoulders relaxed and he let out a big sigh.

"I almost think you are not Dominican, *cara*," he said with a startling smile.

I smiled back at him.

"Okay, let's take a break. I need to think about this," he said.

Papi went back to the porch and I went inside to help Mami and Angela clean up the big mess from the fiesta.

The next day, when I got home from school, Papi was waiting for me on the porch. But there were no bottles or glasses in his hand. And when he said *Hola* to me, there was no smell of rum.

"*¿Qué pasa?*" I asked, suspiciously.

"Change your clothes, *cara*, and let's go."

"Where?" I asked.

"You'll see," said Papi.

I went inside and Mami handed me some shorts, a shirt, and my slippers. "What's going on, Mami?" I asked. "Where is Papi taking me?"

Mami only smiled and said, "You'll see."

As Papi and I set off down the dirt track, Mami waved from the porch.

Questions swirled around and around in my head but I had learned that sometimes no matter how many questions you ask, a grown-up is not going to answer you. "You'll see" are code words for "It's a surprise," and I don't know why they think that we want to be surprised all the time.

Papi and I walked along the road until we got to Sosúa Beach. I love the beach, and this one was the most beautiful of all the beaches on our Island. It is close to my home and the sand is a glorious white that burns your feet in the middle of a sunny day. The sea is blue and the water is so clear that you can see everything on the bottom even when you are up to your neck in water.

"We're going to the beach, Papi?" I asked.

He smiled and nodded. "You love the sea, right?" he asked.

"Yes, Papi, I love the sea more than anything else."

He nodded. "That's what I thought."

I didn't understand but as soon as I saw the water and the waves, I felt happy the way I always do.

When we got to the edge of the water Papi stopped and took off his shoes. "Okay, *cariño*, we're going to feel the music of the sea."

I took off my slippers too and waded into the water.

"No, we're not going in," said Papi. "Come here."

I went over by Papi and looked at him in a puzzle.

"Listen to the sea," said Papi. "Close

your eyes and listen to the sea."

I did what he said. It was easy because I do it all the time. I love all of the sounds of the sea. It's like a special band playing music all its own.

"Do you hear the music, Ana Rosa?" asked Papi.

I nodded. This was no problem at all.

I listened to the booming of the waves on the rocks, and I listened to the whisper of the waves that slipped up to the sand, and I listened to the swooshing of the wind gliding over the water.

Then Papi took my hands in his. "Now keep your eyes closed and let's dance," he said.

At first I felt funny, dancing with my Papi on the beach. But as I listened to the sea I began to feel the music in my feet and in my heart and all around me.

"Papi, I'm dancing," I wanted to shout

as he twirled me in the sand. My hands left his as I turned and turned, and then my hands fell smoothly back into his. My toes slid in and out of the sand left then right, then all around. I was a balloon finally free of its string.

The music of the sea went on and on and Papi and I danced until the sun slipped huge and orange onto the edge of the ocean.

At the end of our dance, beach vendors who were packing up for the day stopped and clapped for us.

Papi held out my hand and I bowed. I couldn't stop giggling as we walked back home. "I can dance!" I wanted to tell everyone we passed.

When we got home, Mami was waiting on the porch with two glasses of lime juice.

Papi winked at her. Mami's face turned red and I laughed. Then Papi turned on the radio and held out his hand to me.

We began to dance, and I slowly felt the *merengue* beat slipping into my Dominican bones just the way it is supposed to. Mami sat on the porch and watched, tapping her foot to the music.

Papi and I danced on as the circle moon filled the sky with light. At that moment, my Papi was everything I had always wanted him to be.

∼

MY
BROTHER'S
FRIEND

I race across the kitchen
jump up on the counter
bruise my knees
on the edge
scrape my arms
tear my dress
hold my heart that beats too loud
strain my eyes as I watch
my brother's best friend
driving up.

His baseball cap's pulled low.
His eyes are hooded dark.
His brown arm rests just perfect
on the door of his car.

I race across the room
jump over chairs and dogs,
hit my elbow
stub my toe
then slide onto the porch.
There he is
my brother's friend
leaning on his car.

I smile at him.
Call his name.
Wave my hand
invite him in.
But all he says
without a glance
is "Hey kid, where's your brother?"

IF THERE WAS ANYTHING THAT distracted me from writing poems and stories every day, it was my brother's best friend, Angel Rodríguez.

Angel had been a part of our family, sitting round our Sunday table for lunch, ever since Guario started working at Roco's Cafe with him two years before.

One day I looked at Angel across the table and saw more than Guario's best friend. Suddenly I couldn't stop thinking about him. My mind, once a pool of words and ideas, was now filled up with images of Angel. My dark eyes trailed him like a line of hot soot wherever he went.

I knew I was in love with Angel because just thinking about him made me feel sick. It was the sickness of wanting something I could never have. Like the books, thick and lovely with words, that I could never hold. Bookstore owners looked at me in my faded school uniform and closed their lips tight as they shook their heads. I might smudge the pages, they said. So I stood, hands behind my back so I wouldn't be tempted, staring at books I couldn't open.

That's how it was with Angel. I stared at his smiling face, his smooth brown muscles, and kept my thoughts behind my back.

Angel and Guario were best friends but they were opposite stars in a galaxy. Whenever Angel came to our home, he laughed out loud and grabbed Mami's hand and danced her around the room.

"Hola, mi amor," he flirted.

He slapped Papi on the shoulder and took a swig of his rum straight from the bottle. He leaned close to Angela and whispered things in her ear that made her clap her hand over her mouth.

"You are *malo*, Angel." My sister giggled behind her hand.

As for me, Angel winked at me carelessly and brushed my hair off my face, sometimes leaning down to kiss my cheek. I trembled fiercely as if a hurricane gale was swooshing through my heart.

"My little *estrella*," Angel called me.

The rest of the day we would all smile at each other more and say things we never would say during the rest of the week. Once I heard Mami tell Papi, "That boy has the perfect name. He sure brings heaven with him."

Some weeks I just could not wait for Sunday to come so I left my gri gri tree after school, shouting to the wide-open windows, "Mami, I'm going for a walk."

I strolled down to Roco's Cafe on the beach and sat on a hard stone wall watching Guario and Angel dance their waiter's dance around the beautiful tourists. I watched as girls whispered their orders, making Angel lean closely over them, his ears touching their hibiscus-red lips. Long smiles and fast winks went back and forth like a volleyball game.

I didn't mind watching all this because I never dared to dream of having Angel—

until the night of Roco's big Christmas fiesta. Every year, on *Nochebuena*, the night before Christmas, Roco has a big fiesta on the patio of his restaurant and everyone is invited, even the families of the waiters. Roco cooks a *lechón asado* over hot coals right on the beach and they say it is the best-tasting roast pig ever. The children get the first chunks of *chicharrones*, crispy pork skin, and it's the best Chistmas present of all.

The singing starts when the midnight stars are bright. Then the chairs are pushed back and the dancing goes on until Christmas Day comes, bright and cheery over the green hills.

Since Papi had taught me to dance, I decided that this would be the best fiesta of all. I would finally stop sitting at the side and I would dance for everyone to see. I would show Angel that I was not just Guario's little sister. I was Ana Rosa, a girl who could dance and dream.

Mami said that she would stay at home. "I have a whole pork leg to get ready and cook."

But we all knew Papi. As soon as that pork leg was finished, he would grab Mami's arm and swing her down to Roco's to dance a couple of *merengues* under the Christmas moon. Provided that he had not drunk more than one bottle of rum and fallen asleep under the porch light instead.

Angela was going, and she began preparing herself a whole week before. She even borrowed a page from my notebook to write down all the things she had to do just to get ready. Every day she checked off something else.

"My nails are done, my legs are shaved, my dress is hemmed," and on and on.

I had never seen Angela so concerned about anything before and I began to wonder about her true plans. But not too much because I was busy trying to get my own self into the best-looking me there ever was. Angel just had to see me as more than Guario's little sister, and that was that!

Finally the day of the fiesta arrived. Mami had made me a beautiful dress from two of Angela's old dresses. My dress had a long, dark green skirt and when I twirled around, it flowed out like ripples in a river pool. The top was white and lacy like the delicate spiderwebs in the branches of my gri gri tree. Mami curled my long brown hair into ringlets down my back. When I walked they swung to and fro like a clock ticking off the minutes. I didn't have fancy dress shoes, only thick brown shoes I wore to school and church or the rubber slippers I wore everywhere else.

Mami tried to stuff tissues into the toes of Angela's old dress-up shoes for me but it didn't work. As soon as I took a step the shoes were left behind on the floor.

Finally I decided that I would wear my slippers and when I got to the party I would take them off and go barefoot.

"That's what the tourist girls do," I told Mami. "They never wear shoes at all."

With a worried look on her face, Mami asked Guario if that was true. He told her it was and she said okay.

Guario whistled when he saw me and spun me around. "*Cariño*, you will break my heart tonight," he said.

Guario looked as if he would break a few hearts himself. He had on his black waiter's pants, but instead of the white T-shirts they usually wore, he had on a long-sleeved white shirt and a red tie. His thick dark hair was brushed back and he looked dashing and handsome.

"All you need is a black mask and I could call you Zorro," I joked.

That was when Angela appeared. There were no words that night for how beautiful my sister looked. Angela's hair was piled on top of her head with curls falling like slow honey down to her shoulders. She had made her dress herself from a piece of precious cloth Mami had brought out of an old suitcase, stashed away there for her eldest daughter since Angela's birth.

The dress was a column of ivory laced with threads of gold and when Angela walked she shimmered like the Christmas angel on top of the tree in Roco's Cafe. There were no flowing ripples in Angela's skirt. There was just Angela and her slim, perfect dress and I had never seen anyone so lovely.

Even Guario was astonished when he took her hand. Papi kept wiping his eyes as if he were seeing a mirage.

"You look just like your Mami when I first met her," he said.

Mami scoffed, "Ha! I was wearing my wash-day clothes, Papi," she said.

"And you looked just like this to me," he replied.

Mami and Papi stood on the porch, their arms around each other. Roberto decided to wait and come later with them, so Guario escorted me and Angela to the party.

We could see the colorful Christmas lights blinking on and off at Roco's Cafe long before we arrived. The night air was warm and laced with the scents of salt, flowers, and excitement.

I saw Angel as soon as we walked in. My heart was tracking double-time to the *merengue* beat filtering through the conversation and laughter.

"Oh my," I whispered to myself. Angel was wearing the exact same clothes as Guario, but on him the white shirt looked like angel wings and his smile was pure heaven. Mami was right after all.

I kicked off my slippers under the edge of a huge tub of flowers and stood silently

waiting for Angel to see me, to see my
grown-up green mermaid dress, to lean his
ear close to my curls so I could whisper
"Feliz Navidad."

But Angel never once looked at me
except to smile quickly and say *"Hola,* little *estrella,"* the same as always, the same as
on Sundays when I was dressed in shorts
and T-shirts with dirty knees and two long
braids.

Angel's dark eyes and his long black
eyelashes rested themselves like butterflies
on my sister and that was it. They stayed
there the rest of the night. Angel and
Angela, two beautiful angels, had become
one.

I walked away in my bare feet, my
green river dress trailing behind me, my
curls swinging back and forth to a soul-sad
rhythm.

"Hey, Cinderella, do you want to
dance?"

Guario stood before me, his hand out-stretched.

"No." I shook my head, and my curls and everything that was in me said it too. "No, thanks."

I walked around looking at all of the food spread out on bright red tablecloths. A nice, smiling woman handed me a bowl of *arroz con dulce* and I tried hard to smile back. I put the tip of the spoon into my mouth and tasted the sweet rice pudding, but even this treat stuck like cement in my mouth.

I saw the huge pig roasting on a spit next to the patio. The lights were so bright I could not see any stars.

I walked over to the stone wall and sat down, swinging my bare legs. I watched Angel dancing with Angela under the Christmas lights. He was so tall and strong as he held my sister close and whispered in her ear. I saw her look up at him with eyes that, if they were mine, would be filled with moonlight and songs.

This was not like looking at books I couldn't touch. This was a whole lot worse. No books or words, no poems or stories—nothing could ever make me feel like this. It was as if I had swallowed a huge mouthful of seawater and couldn't breathe.

"Oh God," I whispered. "I must have dreamed wrong if I feel like this."

I was still sitting on the wall when Guario walked up next to me and handed me a glass of ice-cold Coke. Then he leaned his elbows against the wall. Together we looked at the scene on the patio of Roco's Cafe.

"Everyone loves him; don't feel bad," said Guario.

"I don't," I replied, swallowing the cold drink. I didn't feel like asking Guario how he knew.

"Why do you sit here watching him if it hurts so much?" he whispered.

I sat very still, feeling Guario's words touch me like cold rain.

"How do you know it hurts me?" I asked.

Guario looked at me. "I don't need words to know everything."

"Can anyone else tell?" I asked fearfully.

"Angel can't," he said. "And that's what you really want to know, right?"

I nodded.

"So it hurts and you sit here watching him anyway?" asked Guario.

"Yes." I nodded. "I can't help it."

Guario shook his head and gave a little laugh. "That's what they all say. I thought you would explain it better."

I shrugged my shoulders and the sleeves of my river dress slid down. I yanked them back up.

"Haven't you ever been in love with anyone?" I asked.

"No time for that," he answered quickly. His words slipped down my spine like ice.

"Yes, you have," I argued.

Guario didn't say anything. He just turned his head and looked at the sea.

"I don't need words to know everything either," I said softly, putting my hand on top of his.

Guario and I stayed by the wall—me looking at Angel spreading his cheer all over Roco's Cafe, and Guario looking at the sea.

Somewhere, I knew, there was a girl that my big brother loved. And although he would never admit it, I knew that I was the reason he was not somewhere far away, maybe Canada or Germany or *Nueva* York, with his girl, living his future.

"Maybe you have dreamed wrong,

too," I said at last. "Staying here with us, I mean."

"Never," he answered, and squeezed my hand. "I have you, remember?"

And those were the words that put my broken heart in place—just for a moment. Just long enough for me to smile at my big brother. In his eyes I saw the reflection of the Christmas lights and I had to wonder if not for the bright lights would I see something else there, something Guario wanted no one to see.

It was I who suggested we go back to the party. But I couldn't sing or dance that evening. So I sat next to the tub of red flowers and I waited patiently for Christmas Day to arrive over the green hills. Out of the corner of my eye, I could see Angel and Angela. To stop thinking about them and to keep my belly from hurting so much I thought about my brother Guario instead and his search for his future.

What I didn't know was that my own future was galloping toward me like a riderless horse, and with it were a lot of questions that only I could answer.

ONE SUNDAY

One Sunday, a storm blew in
with green-gold waves
touching the sky
and coconut trees flinging about
dancing with ghost clouds
whispering lies.

And the rain—sharp and white
painting words on the sand
that change my life.
No stars, no moon,
no songs, or stories
to find me and hide me.
No brothers or sister
or Mami or Papi
to hold me and calm me.

The rain words fall in tunnels
leaving dark holes of truth
of who I am.
Who am I?
Remind me please,
before this Sunday storm decides.

S UNDAY WAS THE DAY I LOVED BEST
and the day I feared most. From
the time I was five years old I knew
that on Sundays we were going to the
beach. I also knew that on Sundays, Papi
was going to get drunk—very drunk, no
matter what.

Call it an end-of-the-week celebra-
tion—perhaps that is how Papi and his
friends saw it, but Sunday was reserved for
nothing but drinking and they started at
nine o'clock in the morning. All over the
porch they sat in their white sleeveless

vests, with their thick brown arms slung over the backs of chairs. In the middle of the porch was a rickety table full of bottles of liquid gold shining in the sunlight.

I sat high in my gri gri tree after church waiting for Mami to take me, Roberto, and Angela to Sosúa Beach. We would pack up our white plastic buckets with chicken and gravy and boiled bananas and walk down to the beach. While Mami sat under the shade of an almond tree, Roberto, Angela, and I swam and jumped in the blue waves. Sometimes we would play catch on the beach if we found a stray ball that tourists had left behind.

By the afternoon our friends from school would be on the beach with their families and I would play with them, having speed races on the sand and seeing who could jump the highest to touch the branches of the almond trees.

Sunday was definitely the best day. Mami smiled a lot and Angela took time to teach me things out in the bright sunlight, like how to braid my wet, sandy hair. But as wonderful as Sundays could be, I lived in terror. Because on some Sundays, on too many of them, as a matter of fact, Papi would decide to stroll down the beach to meet us.

By the time Papi arrived on Sosúa Beach, he could hardly walk. He would stumble along, tripping over my friends' towels and baskets. He'd lurch toward me and hug me tightly, saying, "Do you love your Papi? How much do you love your Papi?"

I was always surprised that the sun didn't slip behind a cloud or something to warn me of what was coming. It shone on bright as ever as I clutched Papi to keep him and myself from falling onto the sand.

Finally Roberto would appear to lead Papi over to the almond tree and help him sit next to Mami. She never once uttered a word. Not to him and not to us. She would gaze at the sea with a look on her face that made me think she wasn't even there with us.

From his place next to Mami, Papi would shout at us, demanding that we bring cups of rum and Coke from friends' coolers. Fortified with that, he would shake Mami by the shoulders asking, "*¿Qué pasa, mi amor?*"

Through the years, Sundays began to get worse as Papi demanded louder and meaner, "*¿Qué pasa, mi amor?*" and Mami never answered. As if to show her up, Papi would pull me close and he would ask again and again, "I'm your Papi, right, *cariño*? I'm your Papi?"

"*Claro que sí,*" I would answer. "Of

course yes." And I tried to squirm away from his mutilating breath.

But that wasn't good enough and Papi would ask me again and again. I answered quickly each time, hoping he wouldn't get loud or do as he once did, walking up and down the beach, dragging me along, saying "This is my daughter. MY daughter!"

A few months after I had turned twelve and I had finally learned to dance and braid my hair perfectly and write stories I was proud to read out loud, I found out something that would forever change my Sundays.

I was walking home from school one day when I saw a man dressed all in white sitting on top of a mule with a saddle—a real leather saddle—this was a big *jefe*, that was clear.

The man looked me up and down.

"You are Ana Rosa, sí?" he asked me.

I nodded my head. Before I could ask him who he was he leaned down and handed me a five-peso bill. I examined the red paper in amazement. So much money! I looked at him and he said, "Buy something nice, anything you want. And take your mami her favorite yellow-and-black cake."

I was so surprised that all I could say was *"Gracias, señor."*

I didn't even know Mami had a favorite cake. I watched as the man's sturdy mule carried him down the lane. Then I ran to Señor Garcia's *colmado* and asked for my beloved *dulces*, a handful of *chiclets*, and Mami's yellow-and-black cake. I raced home to show Mami the treats.

Her eyes opened wide when she saw the *dulces* I pulled out of the bag. When I laid the cake on the table and said, "Your favorite!" she grabbed my shoulder roughly.

"Where did you get all this?" Her voice burned like fire in my ears.

My knees began to tremble. Before I could explain about the man on the mule, Mami dragged me across the room and out the door.

"We are going down to the *colmado* right now to find out how you paid for this," she said. "Ana Rosa, I swear if I find out you took money from anyone . . ."

"I didn't steal it, Mami," I cried, walking as fast as I could next to her.

As we walked, I told her about the man on the mule. But the more I talked, the more her face set into a mask of anger. I was scared to look at my Mami because she didn't look like herself anymore. There were no sweet smiles and gentle words. My Mami had walked straight out of herself and left behind a stranger. She was a star that had exploded on earth and was tearing up everything in her path.

When we reached the *colmado*, Mami spoke so swiftly to Señor Garcia that I could hardly understand a word. For five minutes the words fell around me in places I couldn't reach. I gave up trying to gather them into anything sensible.

After a while, Mami took my hand and we walked home. I knew from nothing I had been told but from everything I could feel that our lives had changed.

Before we reached the house, I heard Papi's whistling. It was payday for Guario and we had been getting ready for another little fiesta. Papi was fixing up the porch with chairs. When he heard us walk up he turned around but as soon as he saw Mami's face, he stopped. He stood as still as the leaves before a rainstorm.

Then, in a split second, I saw my

swift-dancing Papi turn into a clumsy old man. His hand reached blindly behind him for a chair. With a heavy sigh, Papi sat down and looked at us with eyes that were two dark holes. Suddenly I felt very frightened.

"*¿Qué pasa*, Mami, Papi?" I asked softly.

I listened as Mami spoke, very slowly this time and very clearly, telling Papi about the man on the mule. About how this man was my father. And how he had given me money and ridden off.

"But I already have a father," I said when Mami was finished. "Right, Papi?"

Papi bent his head and stared into his rum bottle.

Mami wiped her hands on her dress and sat down on the porch. I had never seen Mami sit on the porch during the day—never in my life. That's how I knew she was serious and that the man I was calling Papi was not my Papi. I looked at him—my dancing, smiling, ever-drinking Papi—the man who taught me to dance and who, without fail, embarrassed me on Sundays. The man who insisted I was his daughter—what was Mami saying?

How could the man in white sitting on top of that mule with the fancy leather saddle be my father? Mami kept speaking and in the background of my confusion I heard her words telling me about one Sunday, long ago, when Papi went off for days drinking away all the pesos for food. And she had nothing to feed Guario, Roberto, and Angela.

What was Mami saying—that the man on the mule gave her money? He bought her food? And then he became my father? I knew with all my heart that this did not make any sense. But in my gut, at the very bottom of my confusion, was the fear that

Mami was telling the truth.

I got up and ran, leaving Mami and my not-Papi on the porch. I went down to the beach, the only place in the world for me. I walked past my friends playing at the edge kicking up water and hunching in the trees like tree frogs.

I passed them silently.

"Where you going, Ana Rosa?" they called out.

I walked down the beach searching for quiet, but the sound of the wind and the waves made that impossible.

There was no quiet—it was as loud as if a thousand windows were open and you could hear the voices of all your neighbors.

Questions swirled around in my head, making me dizzy. If Papi was not my father, then did I still have a family? And what about Guario—was he my brother? I felt a sharp pain in my side and I held my waist, bending over with the incredible feeling of loss that Guario might not be my brother. "But he is—he is!" I shouted to the sky.

I closed my eyes against the stinging sun and sat down on the sand. When the sun had filled up all the spaces of my skin with its heat, I stood up and walked into the water, my arms outstretched at my sides. It was so clear that I could see my shadow in the water. I was a dark cross below the surface. The beautiful clear water opened for me and I slipped below, letting the coolness fill me up.

I would never be the same Ana Rosa Hèrnandez again.

When I finally came up for air, I turned on my back and floated, staring at the faraway sky and listening to the sea-music in my ears.

I wished I could stay there forever

surrounded above and below by the blueness of heaven and water. A place where
words did not exist. Nothing but a circle of
darkness spreading inside me.

For some time I floated, gazing at the
sky. Then, from far off, I heard whispery
words. It was a rhyme that I used to sing to
my mother.

Del cielo cayó una rosa	*A rose fell from the sky But it was not destroyed.*
pero no se desajó.	
Mi madre me quiere mucho	*My mother loves me a lot*
pero más la quiero yo.	*But I love her more.*

I closed my eyes to all the blueness
around me and thought about my mother—
my Mami—my wash-day friend—my Stand
up straight and never look down force—my
"You will write stories, *cariño*" believer.

From somewhere inside myself, I knew that Mami needed me and that she had a whole bunch of words and questions fighting her like I did. And if we didn't stick together then one dark night those very same questions would eat us up and spit our bones across the sand.

But I was a writer, wasn't I? I loved words. To me, Papi was *still* my Papi and words didn't have to be the enemy destroying my family. I had a power over them.

I could make words into anything I wanted. Not lies, not tales of sorrow, but the opposite. I could rewrite everything to make my not-Papi's Sunday eyes disappear and maybe bring my Mami's faraway Sunday face back to us . . . to him.

One girl's words, I thought, can they be that powerful? It was time to find out. I would write a poem, I decided, and I would give it to Mami and Papi and they would know then how words are everything and nothing all at the same time. Because the man on the porch drinking his rum is my Papi, whether I like him or not—he is my Papi, and the man on the mule is a story!

∽

THE COLORS OF POWER

It's an election year.
The loudspeakers blare.
The colors of the candidates
are painted everywhere.
Purple for one, Red for another.
White for the man my mother cheers.

The colors of power painted on rocks,
on lampposts, and trees and passing trucks.
Fiesta balloons, and merengue *tunes*
sweet promises, smiles and silvery moons.
All is a show with colors so clear
That shimmer and fling our hopes in the air.

But beware of them, I warn!
These colors of power.

I FEARED THAT OUR FAMILY WOULD NO longer be the same after finding out about the man on the mule. But I didn't have to worry too long. At first there was a lot of silence between Mami and Papi and even between Angela and Mami. But nobody treated me any different. Guario even shook my ponytail and told me that I better not get any funny ideas in my head because "you're the very same Ana Rosa as ever," he testified.

Roberto said, "There was never a question about that, big brother."

That made me smile a lot and when Mami took my special poem I had written about Papi and taped it to the fridge, I saw Papi and Angela and Mami reading it many times during the day and smiling at each other more and more. But what really broke the silence and put the man on the mule far from everyone's minds was the news that the government wanted to buy our land.

The people who lived in my village had lived there so long they could not remember who built the first house or where one person's property lines stopped and another's began. That was the whole point—we all lived side by side, neighbors, friends, sharing, and no one giving a shake of the head to what some big-mouth politician was suddenly saying about dividing up our land.

"Foreign investors!" "Money for the Island!" "Improvements!" "Progress!" The man stood on a makeshift stage, the back of a pickup truck, with a megaphone in hand announcing to us as if he were reading out the lottery numbers.

After the first few words, the children went back to playing and feeding the clucking chickens that circled the black truck. Me, I climbed right up my gri gri tree to watch in case something interesting was going to happen.

Nothing did. But later that evening I sat at our kitchen table and listened as Papi told Guario what the man had said. Papi slammed down his glass of rum and Coke more than a few times in between the telling, and Mami kept shaking her head and mumbling "Dios Mío" under her breath, so I knew something bad was going on.

But Guario didn't seem worried. "They can't make us leave our homes," he said slowly, as if explaining the ABCs to Mami and Papi.

"Everybody here, all our families have lived on this land for more than the amount of years needed to own it. We are the owners of this land. They can't sell it unless we let them. It's the law!"

Guario was so sure about this that when the neighbors gathered on our porch later to talk and talk about it, they appointed him the official spokesperson.

"Guario, you talk to this *loco* man and tell him we don't want to sell," said Papi.

"Well," interrupted Mami, "some people might want to sell; we don't know that."

Then Señor Garcia spoke up. "I am sure that if someone wants to buy they want to buy it all, not a piece here and a piece there."

It was agreed that our whole village would join together to announce that we weren't interested in selling.

So Guario met with the government man, Mr. Moreno. He reported that Mr. Moreno had shaken his head during the entire conversation and at the end, Mr. Moreno's answer was that he had bigger fish to fry.

"What's that mean?" demanded Papi.

Guario shrugged but there was a worried frown on his face.

For the next few weeks we all forgot

about Mr. Moreno and went about our business. It was an election year and the grown-ups were busy making signs and holding "talks" and the teenagers were busy going around with cans, painting up everything they could find in the colors of their favored candidates.

Soon the whole of Sosúa and my village were blooming purple, red, and white rocks, fences, palm trees, and walls. Nothing was safe from the painters, who were said to be armed by the government men themselves with innumerable paint cans.

The people were also coming up with slogans and hand signals to identify each candidate so that wherever you went in the streets, people were giving each other their signal, and a hail of cheers would erupt.

Me, I didn't pay it too much attention. I went to school and helped Mami and Angela in the house and wrote in my notebooks that Guario gave me. I was close to putting away my longing for Angel and accepting the idea of Angela and Angel as *novios*.

The fact is, I had bigger fish to fry too. I was busy being as much me as possible, given the recent news that I was someone else. And, more important, my thirteenth birthday was coming up and I knew Guario, Mami, Papi, and even Roberto and Angela were planning a special surprise.

"What is it?" I begged them to tell me.

But they said, "Just wait, *cariño*, you'll see."

I didn't dare to hope for anything, and the truth is that anything would have been great because I had never gotten a birthday surprise before. There was never money for presents—at least not regular-type presents wrapped in paper and bows.

Instead, on birthdays, Papi might make you a sand sculpture that was so perfect you didn't want the sea to ever wash it away. Or Mami might bake a special cake with lots of real frosting, or we might have a day to do whatever we wanted, like stay on the beach until the stars came out—which was almost always my choice.

I began preparing for my new year by writing in my notebook all of the things I had learned while I was twelve and all the things I wanted to accomplish during thirteen. I wrote about how I could dance *salsa* and *merengue* and write poems and stories to read aloud and how my Papi was even more special than before.

Then I wrote about how I wanted to learn to windsurf like Roberto and the boys on Cabarete Beach. I wanted to learn English better and I wanted to write more poems and stories. And most of all I wanted to help Guario to find his future.

This one was the hardest but it was always on my mind. Once I asked Guario what that meant—a future—and he said,

"It's something special you do with your life."

I wanted to tell Guario that he was already doing something special with his life by being my brother, but I didn't think he would count that.

Deep down I believed that Guario felt he had to live up to the great Taíno chief he was named after—Guarocuya. From the time I was little, Mami used to tell us the story of Guarocuya, who had defied the Spanish conquistadors and conquered them in battle after battle, disguising himself as a rock, a tree, or a river until eventually the King and Queen of Spain wanted to give him a title. But Guarocuya said No, he did not want a title, just freedom.

The Spanish said, Okay you can have freedom, but what they didn't realize was that Guarocuya had it all along, it wasn't something for them to give. And Guarocuya lived all his days in total freedom. It was the same with my brother. Just as Guarocuya fought so hard for freedom, my brother was fighting for a future.

When Mr. Moreno showed up again on the back of his pickup truck, everyone in our village thought the same thing: "Where's Guario?"

Papi sent Roberto down to Roco's Cafe to fetch him. In the meantime, Mr. Moreno was handing out pieces of paper to the people. Mami and Papi got one and began shaking their heads. There were groans from the women and the men were muttering all sorts of bad words under their breath.

Guario came striding up, his face glistening with sweat.

Everyone moved back to let him walk through the crowd to the truck, and along the way someone put one of the leaflets in his hands.

Well, I have to say that I had never seen

Guario's face get so dark and angry in my life as it did when he read it.

Before Guario could say a word, Mr. Moreno held up his hands and started talking through his megaphone.

There were a lot of words I didn't understand but the ones I did scared me to death. Words like The government owns this land; and The government has the right to sell it to whomever it wants; and The government is selling it now to a big company for them to build hotels, and this would benefit everyone with more jobs and more tourists. But everyone would have to move immediately. That was what I understood and that was enough.

I ran as fast as I could over to my gri gri tree and climbed up. High in the green leaves, I could still see the man and hear his voice, but now he was just a speck far below and he was not as scary. I felt much better. I wondered if perhaps Guarocuya felt the same way from on top of his mountain—he could look down on the Spaniards and feel they weren't so scary from way up high.

Well, I was glad I was up in my gri gri tree because this time plenty of things happened. Guario held up his leaflet and tore it slowly in half right in front of Mr. Moreno's face. Then he tossed the pieces carelessly into the back of the pickup, as if they were nothing but trash.

On that gesture the history of our neighborhood pivoted. Before that we were a frightened village afraid of losing our land. After that we became a village of rebels fighting to keep our homes. Mr. Moreno just stared at Guario at first, then he picked up his megaphone. But no one could hear a word because we all began booing him.

Then, one by one, each man and woman, and even the children, began tearing their leaflets in half and throwing the pieces into the truck.

Mr. Moreno kept wiping his brow. When everyone quieted down he raised his megaphone again and said, "I understand how you feel and your President understands too. Believe me, he is doing this for you. With new hotels, there will be more and better jobs for all of you. There will be more tourism, more money for everyone."

"We want our homes!" shouted someone.

Then Guario spoke up.

"Mr. Moreno," he said loud and clear, "we are not moving from the homes and from the land that belongs legally to our families."

The people cheered. Mr. Moreno shook his head. "The land is already sold!" he shouted.

There was complete silence. Mr. Moreno barely made it back inside his pickup truck as his driver revved up the engine. But the government men couldn't go anywhere because a bunch of people had moved in front of the truck. Some boys began jumping on the bumper and shaking the truck. Mr. Moreno rolled up his windows. Others began hitting the sides of the truck with sticks.

The truck eased its way slowly down the road and when, at last, it turned out of our neighborhood, it was still being followed and booed.

On our porch that night, everyone had questions and no one had any answers. Someone suggested we go to the Courts.

"Too corrupt," Señor Garcia said. "We'd never win because all the judges are on the President's side."

"But where will we move to?" cried Señora Garcia.

This was the fear that was on everyone's

mind. These homes were all we had. I knew for certain that there was nowhere for my family to go, no relatives who could take us in, no money to buy a home or land anywhere else, nothing.

Finally Guario came up with an idea. He told us that the government would not listen to anything we said unless it affected its own interests. And now that we were so close to an election, the government's main interest was to look good to its citizens.

"We could spread the word throughout the Island of what the government wants to do to us. And maybe we can convince enough people that if we don't all stand up for this, then no one's property will be safe on the Island."

Mami was shaking her head. "If they find out you are behind this, Guario . . ."

"Mami," he said, "we are all behind it."

And everyone on our porch, all the families whom I have known since I was born, said, Yes, we were all in it together.

And so our small rebellion began. But we had no idea it was a rebellion at all. We were just a bunch of neighbors who wanted to keep the same houses where we had lived and our parents had lived and our grandparents had been born. As for me, I mostly wanted to keep my gri gri tree.

For the next two weeks, I watched and listened to everything. When there were meetings I sat on the floor next to Guario's chair and felt comforted by his leg touching my shoulder. Everything would be okay.

The people asked me to write an article, which could be sent to the newspapers. Guario spoke and I wrote down his words. Then I fixed it up so it read like a real story with a beginning and a middle but with no end. Instead I put a question: "What will they do next?"

Someone typed up the article at an

office and made hundreds of copies. It was amazing to see something I had written look so neat and official.

Everyone liked the article except for Mami. When she saw it, she started to cry and I knew it was because of those rocks in the river she was afraid of. The ones that I was supposed to slip softly over until I got out to that big sea, far from our Island.

"It's all right, Mami," I said. "We have to do this."

"No, *cariño*," she whispered, "not you. You are to write lovely poems and stories, remember?"

I hated making Mami so unhappy. I felt guilty walking through the house and seeing her worried eyes following me as if she thought I would disappear tomorrow.

I couldn't explain to Mami that although I loved writing poems much better, I had to write this article instead. I wanted Guario to be proud of me. Deep down I wasn't writing the article for any other reason. And it made me sad to realize I would hurt Mami to show off for Guario.

I tried to argue with myself and say this wasn't true. Guario had told us that our words were all we had since our legal ownership of the land came from possession and not sales papers.

"We must fight them with our words," he had told us.

"And that's what I am doing," I said to myself.

When the three daily newspapers printed my article almost word for word, Mami stopped speaking and became a silent shadow slipping in and out of the spaces of our lives, which were now completely consumed with our battle.

Then reporters came to see us and they took pictures of Guario and our homes and wrote stories that had the finest words I had ever read. They described Guario as a perfect leader of his people. They said he was the future for all of us Dominicans because he showed us how to stand up and fight.

It was clear to me, even if not to Guario, that his future was right here in front of his face and not some far-off idea he might have had. Guario didn't need a future—he *was* the future!

While I was thinking these lofty thoughts, Guario was very busy. He still went to work every day at Roco's Cafe, but whenever he wasn't at work he was making speeches to groups at factories around Puerto Plata, or traveling to Santiago, Santo Domingo, and Samaná to talk to the people.

On the night before my thirteenth birthday, after a long meeting on our front porch, I couldn't sleep so I went into the kitchen to write in my notebook. All talk about my birthday surprise, which Guario and the family had been planning, had stopped in the middle of our crisis. I no longer expected anything special to happen on my birthday. I would be lying if I said that I didn't mind. I did.

I found Guario sitting at the table with his head in his hands. I thought he was asleep, but when I shook his shoulder I saw that he was just staring at his hands.

I sat next to him. I didn't mind that we didn't speak. Next to Guario, I felt safe and sound so words were just extras.

He kept on looking at his hands as I wrote in my notebook. After a while he raised his head and spoke. "They're coming tomorrow."

"Who?" I asked, holding my pen in midair.

"The engineers building the hotel. They're coming tomorrow to start their measurements. And they're coming with the *guardia*."

"But how can they?" I asked. "Everyone is on our side. The newspapers, the workers, practically everybody on the North Coast."

Guario nodded his head tiredly. "Yes, yes, yes."

"Then what happened?" I whispered, a ball of fear forming in my belly.

"Our words aren't enough," he answered. "We are just soldiers of words, and them, they have everything—money and contracts, and bulldozers and guns."

"But words can do anything; you said so yourself!"

"I was wrong. It's people who can do anything." Guario sounded worn out. "Words are just the inventions of people, and they stand for nothing but what people decide they'll be."

I looked at Guario. Was this my brave big brother speaking? The one who told us we must fight with words, was he giving up?

My heart fell a thousand feet and I wanted to shake his shoulders and shout "NO! NO! NO! It's words that can get people to do anything. Words are better than any bulldozer or gun."

But all I said was "So what do we do now?"

"We protect our homes," he answered.

"How?" I demanded.

"The only other way," he said, "when words stop working."

All kinds of things flew through my head. Was he talking guns? No way, I said to myself. No way Guario would talk guns. Then what?

I was so busy being angry that I almost didn't hear him whisper, "Oh God, Ana Rosa, I hate what we're going to do. This should not happen."

The agony I heard in his voice sucked me under. I felt as if I had been slammed by a wave, straight into dark sand. It was like both of us were drowning and the waves were rushing higher and higher over our heads. And neither Guario nor I had any control over what would happen next.

In the morning Guario looked different than the man I had left at the kitchen table the night before. Guario stood tall and strong. His brown eyes reflected the light of the early morning sun as he looked steadily at the villagers from on top of our porch wall. The neighbors stood before him, holding everything from broomsticks and mop handles to rocks, broken-edge bottles, and truck tires.

"Look around you," he said. "This is what you are fighting for today—your family, your homes, your past, and—the start of our futures! Let's pray for understanding instead of indifference, friends instead of enemies, generosity instead of selfishness. And most important, words instead of violence!"

The neighbors cheered and whistled and shouted, *"Sí! Sí!"* Then Guario's voice softened and the crowd quieted down to hear every word.

"We will fight for what is rightfully ours. And we will not give up!"

Every single person standing before Guario on that bright morning nodded his or her head in agreement. We all knew there was nothing more to say. We had to see what would happen next.

Journalists from the local newspapers squatted around the porch, scribbling down Guario's words. The crowd of villagers broke apart to go to their places. Guario passed me on the porch. "Happy Birthday, *cariño*," he said. "Tonight I'm taking you out for an ice cream."

I wanted to hug Guario. I wanted to throw my arms around his shoulders and never let him go into the road in front of everyone who was waiting for him as their leader. I wanted to say "Let's go for an ice cream right now."

But instead I smiled a tiny smile. My mouth could barely move. And I squeezed his hand.

Guario walked away and everything began happening fast. Papi and his *amigos* went to the porch next door lugging black truck tires and cans of gasoline. Mami called me and Angela inside and closed the windows and doors tight. She knelt down on the floor in front of our Virgin Mary statue and began praying. Angela sat on a chair, clutching her knees, her eyes closed tightly.

I listened to Mami recite the holy rosary, and watched as her fingers moved from bead to bead. The words had a nice familiarity and quietness to them.

At eight o'clock, I heard the heavy roar of trucks groaning down our dirt road. It was the engineers and workers. I knew it was them by the noise that started to swell outside—the boos and curses.

Mami was saying her rosary louder to drown out the noises outside and Angela's eyes were shut tight. I made a mad dash for the backdoor. I slipped the latch and ran out. I almost stopped when I smelled the anger in the air.

Boom! An explosion rocked the ground and a cloud of black smoke rose into the sky. I covered my head and ran like a lizard low and fast straight to my gri gri tree. I scuttled up, ripping my hands and feet on the branches.

I didn't dare to look down until I was safe up high. Then, when I did look down, everything was crazy.

Papi and Señor Garcia were pouring gasoline on the truck tires and lighting them with matches. Flames shot into the air. The government workers scampered off the trucks, coughing and waving the smoke from their faces. The scent of burning rubber filled my head as the smoke rose like gray balloons into the sky. When the smoke cleared a little, I saw them—the *guardia*—in their green uniforms, with their long black guns slung across their shoulders on straps.

The *guardia* were shouting and swinging their guns from side to side as if they were performing a dance. On the other side stood my family and neighbors— Señor Garcia, Señor Rojas, Papi, and Guario in the front. They were armed with stones and bats and broken bottles with edges gleaming green through the haze.

I froze when one *guardia* in a red cap poked Guario in his chest with the end of his gun. Guario pushed it away with his hand and shouted something at the fat *guardia*. I gripped the branches so tightly that I couldn't feel my fingers after a while.

Then there was a rumbling sound and the trucks started backing up. They backed up all the way down our dirt road and disappeared around the corner by Señor Garcia's *colmado*. Papi and Señor Garcia and Señor Rojas began slapping each other on the back and clapping. I didn't clap. My eyes were on the fat *guardia* and Guario because they had not moved an inch. They were standing just a few feet away from each other now and almost right below my tree.

My tree began to shake. I could feel it all the way through. The ground was moving. The people below got completely quiet. Everyone heard it at the same time—the sound of mighty engines, roaring slowly toward us.

Slow and steady the loud rumble came. Then big, earth-shaking, ground-eating, yellow-and-black monsters appeared. They devoured everything in their paths. Bushes, flowers, Señor Garcia's *colmado*, trees, porches, and on and on—two giant bull-dozers with mean, hungry jaws.

Señor Garcia tried to run toward his store and home, but the *guardia* pushed him down on the ground. One *guardia* hit Señor Garcia on his head and Papi and Señor Rojas pulled Señor Garcia away before the *guardia* could hit him again. Papi and Señor Rojas shouted and pushed the *guardia*. Mami and Angela opened our windows and screamed when they saw the bulldozers. They ran outside, pulling little children by their hands from neighbors' doors and windows, shoving them out of the way of the bulldozers, which crawled over houses like giant lizards. There were piles of pink and blue and purple rubble left behind—the bricks of once-upon-a-time houses.

The people of my village, both the men and the women, the neighbors who had listened to my story and clapped for me, all turned to face the bulldozers and the *guardia*. With Papi and Guario in front and Señor Rojas and Señor Garcia right next to them, my people began throwing anything they could find—rum bottles and stones, broken bricks from houses no longer standing—anything. Even little children were crying and throwing small stones at the *guardia* and the bulldozers. I watched everything as if it were a dream. I couldn't get down from my tree even if I wanted to.

The bulldozers reached the crowd. Guario put his fingers in his mouth and whistled loudly. Out of the bushes came Roberto and his friends, who rented out beach chairs on Sosúa Beach. Roberto jammed a tree branch into the jaws of a bulldozer. Then he and the beach guys climbed all over the bulldozer like ants swarming a piece of cake. When they dragged the driver out, the first gunshots started.

My eyes swung from one fight to another, from one scream to another, from one gunshot to another. But always, always my eyes rushed back to Guario.

And then everything got still, so still that I could hear the flowers and plants crying. I could hear the sun breathing. And the sea, the beautiful blue sea fell quiet and not one wave rose up. It was all flat and still.

Guario was standing below my gri gri tree, his arms spread wide. A hungry, nasty bulldozer was heading straight for my tree. Guario looked up at me, a worried look on his face. The fat *guardia* in the red cap was pushing his gun at Guario, trying to get him to move away from the tree, but Guario wouldn't budge. I looked down at them from up high in my gri gri world.

"Guario, run," I wanted to shout. But the words couldn't come out. Nothing came out and I just sat there gripping my branch. Then I heard a sound inside my head and I saw Guario's body jerk back. "No!" I shouted. "No!" But even those words didn't come out. They were trapped inside of me where all my fear lives. And as Guario fell at the bottom of my gri gri tree, he looked up and my handsome, brave brother smiled at me. I saw his hands open and they were covered in blood. And suddenly, the volume of the world was turned back on and every noise imaginable fell down upon me. I looked down at Guario laying on the ground below my gri gri, his arms spread wide like angel wings, and that's when I knew it was all my fault.

∽

THE COLOR OF MY WORDS

Silver words
pour down from the sky.
Blue ones float
by and by.
Stir them with red
instruments of blood.
Paint them on white
frame them with mud.
This portrait of magic
held in my hands,
a collage of words
colors and plans.
My brother's story
remembered and told.
The color of my words
forever bold.

FOR DAYS NO ONE COULD GET ME down from my tree. Not that many people tried. Mami had disappeared into her shadow and was hiding in our house somewhere. Papi and Roberto were down at the jail with the other men, answering questions. Angela was sick in her bed.

It was Angel who came and stood at the bottom of my tree and talked to me. For hours he would stay there and sometimes he pulled over Papi's porch chair and sat down next to my gri gri. I never said a word but Angel stayed there anyway. And I think that it must have been Guario asleep in his grave at the bottom of my gri gri who kept Angel company, because it sure wasn't me.

I sat in my tree but I didn't look at anything, not the sea or the mountains. And I didn't feel anything. I didn't even feel the green leaves stirring against me hard when a rainstorm was coming. I got completely wet holding on to a branch as the winds blew, but I didn't feel the chill.

Only at nights I came down from my tree. I walked to the beach and there was only the smooth black sea at midnight when the stars had fallen out of the sky and there was no moon to show that anyone or anything existed here on my Island.

Some nights I climbed into the bed and went to sleep next to Angela. In the mornings I went straight back up into my gri gri tree and started over. I didn't go to school. I didn't talk. I didn't write one word. But there were plenty of words swirling around and around in my head and although I couldn't see what they were, I saw only a haze of color and the color of my words was red.

And then one morning, when I was climbing the tree, a loud noise rang out over the village. It might have been a motorcycle backfiring. But it sounded exactly like the gunshots I had heard on my birthday. I was halfway up the tree and the noise scared me so much that I let go of the branch and fell to the ground.

I saw everything plain as day. The fat *guardia* standing with the gun in his hand. And Guario's blood-hot body at the bottom of my tree.

I put my head down and cried. I cried until all the red had disappeared and I could see only black spaces.

"No more words," I whispered into the ground. I clutched two fistfuls of dirt and looked up at heaven and God and Guario. "I promise I won't write another word!" It was the only punishment I could think of worthy of what I had done. I had sat in my tree and watched my brother die. He was trying to protect me and I had done nothing to help him.

Whether giving up writing even mattered to God or Guario, I did not know.

But it was all I had, and now I didn't have
it anymore, just like I didn't have Guario
anymore, just like I didn't have anything,
nothing at all anymore on my dark green
island where rivers flow swift over hard
rocks.

I didn't even have my gri gri tree anymore. I knew in my heart that I would
never be comfortable in that tree again.
And when I was finally able to open my
eyes and look around, a lot had changed.
The shootings and rioting were over. The
hotel project was called off and the government gave us back our land. That's what
they told the journalists. But they didn't
realize that it wasn't theirs to take or to give
back. We had it all along and had never
given it up—not one inch—because of
Guario.

Angel was going away to *Nueva* York.
Papi and Roberto had come back home
from jail and Papi had a job at the cheese

factory in Sosúa. Angela was cooking din-
ner and taking care of everyone. And
Mami was fitting herself slowly back into
her body.

I tried to tell Mami and Papi that it
was my fault Guario was killed. But Mami
covered her face with her hands and
cried.

"It is all of our fault, *cariño*," she said.

And Papi came over to us and put his
heavy arms on our shoulders and said
softly, *"Cállate, mi amor.* It is not our
fault." But his voice broke in half just like
my heart and even Papi could not convince
me of what I knew was true.

One day I woke up and I realized I was
thirteen years old. It was really six months
after my official birthday, but Papi and
Mami had decided that I would have the
birthday we had all missed. I was not too
happy about it, but it made the whole rest

of the family and even our neighbors ex-
cited. So I pretended it was a great idea.

The day was hot and rain trickled
down from the clouds in bright sunshine
showers. It was the kind of hot where your
blouse sticks to your skin and your hair
curls heavy down your back like jungle
vines.

Outside, banana leaves, broad and
green, waved against the windows. Señor
Garcia waved *Hola* to me as he opened the
doors of his new *colmado* on the corner.
Señor Rojas shouted *Feliz Cumpleaños* to
me as he hurried off to catch a *motoconcho*
to work. Señora Perez came by and gave
me a painting she had painted just for me,
she said. It was Guario, with angel wings
on his back, sitting at the bottom of my gri
gri tree. I bit my lip to not cry in front of
her. It was beautiful and I wondered how
Señora Perez knew this was exactly what I
saw whenever I looked at my tree.

Papi was getting ready for his shift at the cheese factory. No more porch-rum days for him ever since Guario died. Mami told me to look for the good that comes out of the bad. I was the one who sat on the porch after school in Papi's old chair instead.

Every day I sat there and our hot Dominican sun darkened my feet as they rested on the porch wall. My toes pointed straight toward my gri gri tree and the fine white cross that Papi and Roberto had put on Guario's grave.

Our town had changed in six months. It was high tourist-season and there were more tourists than ever before. Hundreds of them came on fat silver planes. They walked around Sosúa in bathing suits, trying out Spanish words with their strange accents.

There was excitement every week when the planes arrived, as if we were all waiting for something big, but we didn't quite know what it was. More tourists is what we got and that was fine because our hotels and restaurants needed them and they made our beaches look happy and full of life. But still we waited for something special to come out of the sky, or maybe it was just me who was waiting.

The morning of my birthday, Papi and Mami gave me the most extraordinary present I will ever get in my life: a gleaming silver-and-blue typewriter and with it, hundreds of sheets of white paper. I stared at it for so long that Papi asked, "*¿Qué pasa, cariño?*"

I shook my head. "Nothing, Papi."

And then I touched it. I ran my hand over the cool metal and stroked the smooth white keys. It was the most beautiful thing I had ever seen.

There was a card and everyone's name was on it. Angel in *Nueva* York, Angela,

Roberto, Papi and Mami, Señor and Señora Garcia, and at the very last was Guario's name in tiny letters so I could hardly read it.

"He told us that you would need this for your future and that we must all work together to get it for you," said Mami.

"When?" I asked, raising my eyes and looking into hers.

Papi cleared his throat. He placed a rough hand on my head. "A few days before he died, *cariño*. He told us you must be a writer. And we promised him."

"But I don't write anymore," I whispered. But that was only partly true. In my head, I had a million stories that wouldn't go away.

Mami spoke sharply. "Well, Ana Rosa, it is time for changes."

I couldn't explain to Mami and Papi why I couldn't write anymore. So I walked down to the beach instead.

It is hard to be unhappy at the beach. The waves talk to you and the wind tickles your neck and the sun-warmed sand flows over your feet, pulling you down, making it harder and harder to walk, forcing you to stop and kick some up, dragging you to the edge where the sand is dark and cool and squishes up tiny stars between your toes.

And there, the waves can get you, splash you with their drops of crystals and make you smile. Then, before you know it, you just run right into the water and splash a big wave straight to heaven where you know your brother is watching. So you smile up at him and you wave if no one is looking and you say "It's my birthday," real soft so no one but the fish can hear you. You wonder for a moment if Guario is listening, but you know he is because he is your brother and he always will be no matter what.

Another wave rises up and splashes you

hard so that your mouth is full of salty water and you spit it out and laugh at the mess you are with your clothes soaking wet and your hair full of sand. But that's okay because it's your birthday.

If ever you will be forgiven for something it is here at the beach under the sun, in the sea, beneath a wave, close to everything that makes you happy without even trying. Words flow like the ocean, like the river on wash day, like Guario's blood on my birthday, his deathday, the same day, the same moment, two tied together forever.

Words, solid like diamonds, plop themselves down in my head and they can't be blocked with rocks or guns or wishes or tears. Words to tell Guario's story.

I look up at the sky and the blue blue faraway heaven where Guario watches me.

"I'm sorry!" I shout as loud as I can. "I'm sorry!" My words are carried off by the waves and the wind. Carried straight to heaven, I hope, where Guario can hear me.

Maybe it's the silver wings on the waves that touch me brand-new, or maybe it's because I have just waited long enough for the answer, but suddenly as I stand there surrounded by ocean and sky, I realize what it is I have to do.

I have to write Guario's story down so that everyone will know my brother. I shall write it all down on my new typewriter. Today is the day I have to start. It is today or never. I know it. So I race out of the waves and run along the beach. And all the way home, words sing in my head.

～